BRUCE WHATLEY

THAT
MAGNETIC
DOG

For Rosie

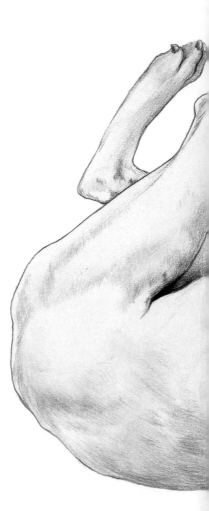

Angus&Robertson
An imprint of HarperCollins*Children'sBooks*, Australia

First published in Australia in 1994
This paperback edition published in 1995
by HarperCollins*Publishers* Pty Limited
ABN 36 009 913 517
harpercollins.com.au

HarperCollins*Publishers*
Level 13, 201 Elizabeth Street, Sydney NSW 2000, Australia
Unit D1, 63 Apollo Drive, Rosedale, Auckland 0632, New Zealand
A 53, Sector 57, Noida, UP, India
1 London Bridge Street, London, SE1 9GF, United Kingdom
2 Bloor Street East, 20th floor, Toronto, Ontario M4W 1A8, Canada
195 Broadway, New York NY 10007, USA

National Library of Australia Cataloguing-in-Publication entry:

Whatley, Bruce.
That magnetic dog.
ISBN 978 0 2071 8365 2 (hbk.)
ISBN 978 0 2071 8420 8 (pbk.)
1. Dogs – Juvenille fiction. I. Title.
A823.3

Colour reproduction by Graphic Print Group, Adelaide
Printed and bound in China by RR Donnelley on 128gsm Matt Art

16 15   18 19

BRUCE WHATLEY

THAT MAGNETIC DOG

Angus&Robertson
An imprint of HarperCollins*Children'sBooks*

Magnets attract metal objects
like keys and spoons.

My dog Skitty
doesn't attract metal.

She attracts food.

When Mum has a biscuit with her tea,
Skitty gives her that look …
that magnetic look.

Before you know it
Skitty has a biscuit too.

Sometimes more than one.

That magnetic look
can be very strong.

We're not allowed to feed Skitty.
at the dinner table

But somehow, food always
goes in her direction.

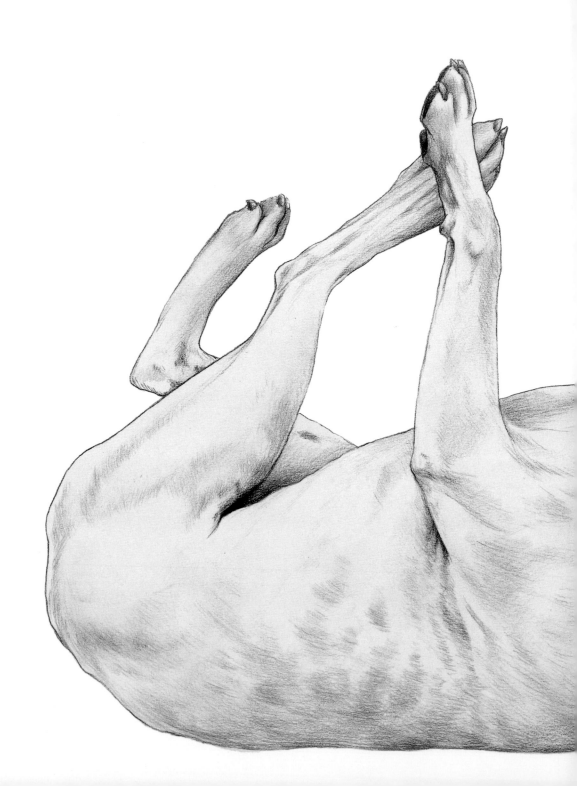

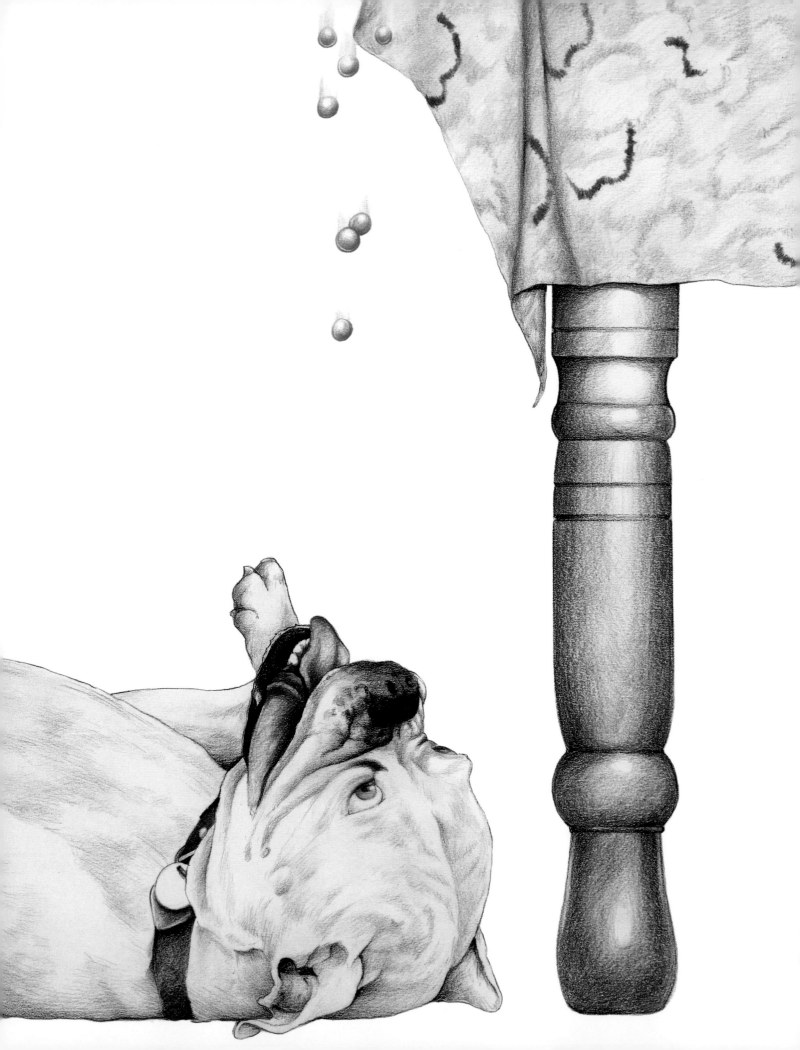

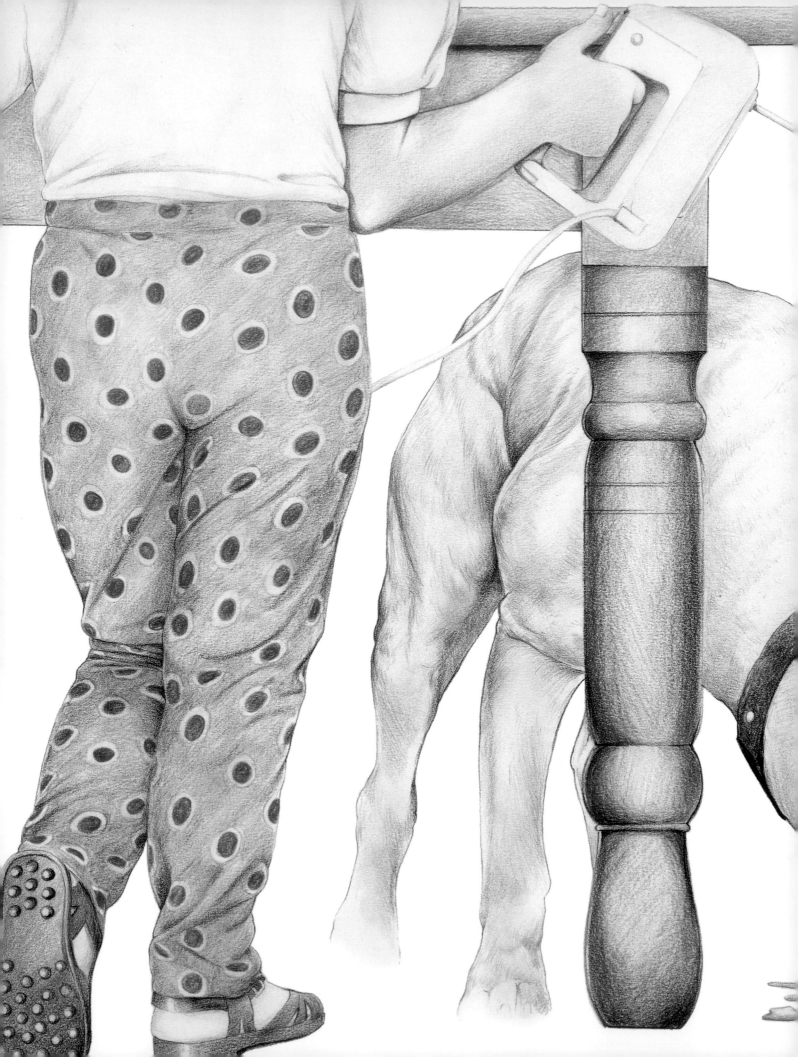

When Dad and I make a cake
we don't worry about any batter
that spills on the floor.

We know it will disappear.

And we never ask,
'Who wants the last bit.'
Skitty always gets the last bit.

Sometimes, she even
gets the first bit!

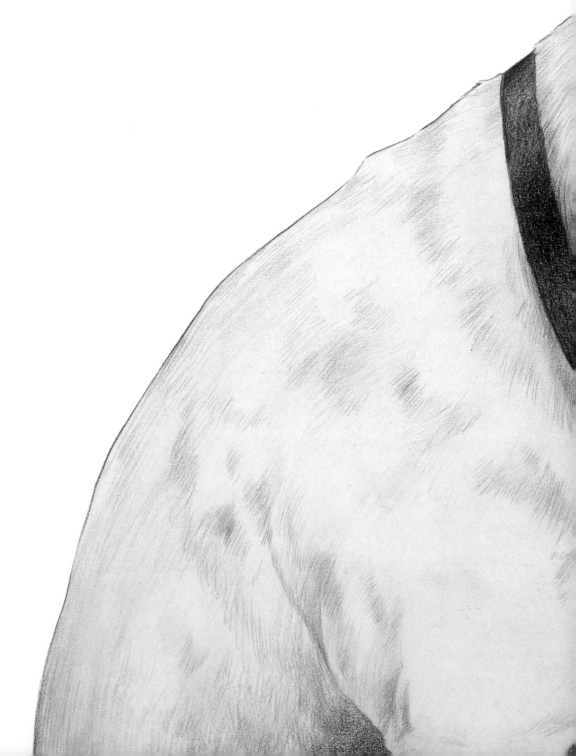

Not that Skitty steals food.
She doesn't have to.

It just seems to follow her around.

Even when Skitty
is walking down the street
food is attracted to her.

She likes Chinese food too
but I wonder if she gets too much of it.

Skitty takes food very seriously.

We have to be extremely fast
when buying fast food.
Blink, and she's taken away
our take-away.

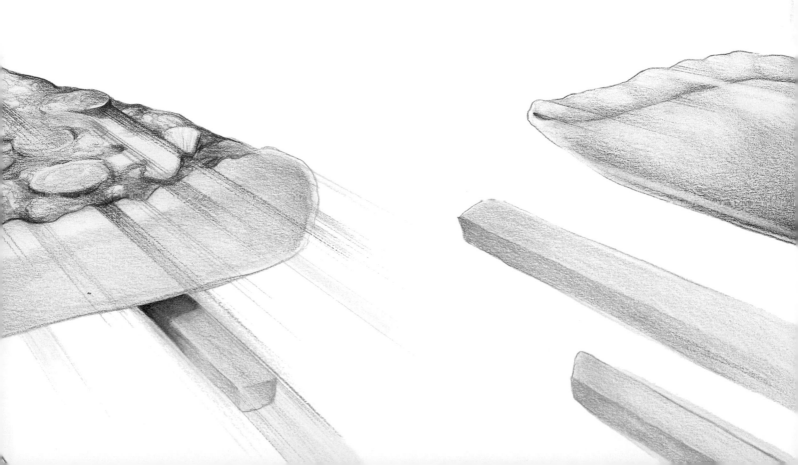

Peanut butter and honey sandwiches
are my favourite.

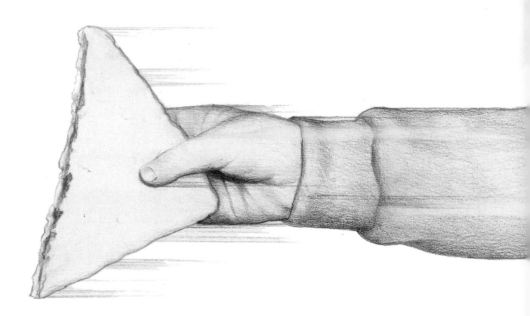

Unfortunately, they're Skitty's too.

Once my brother even climbed our tree
to eat his strawberries in peace.

But there's no escape…

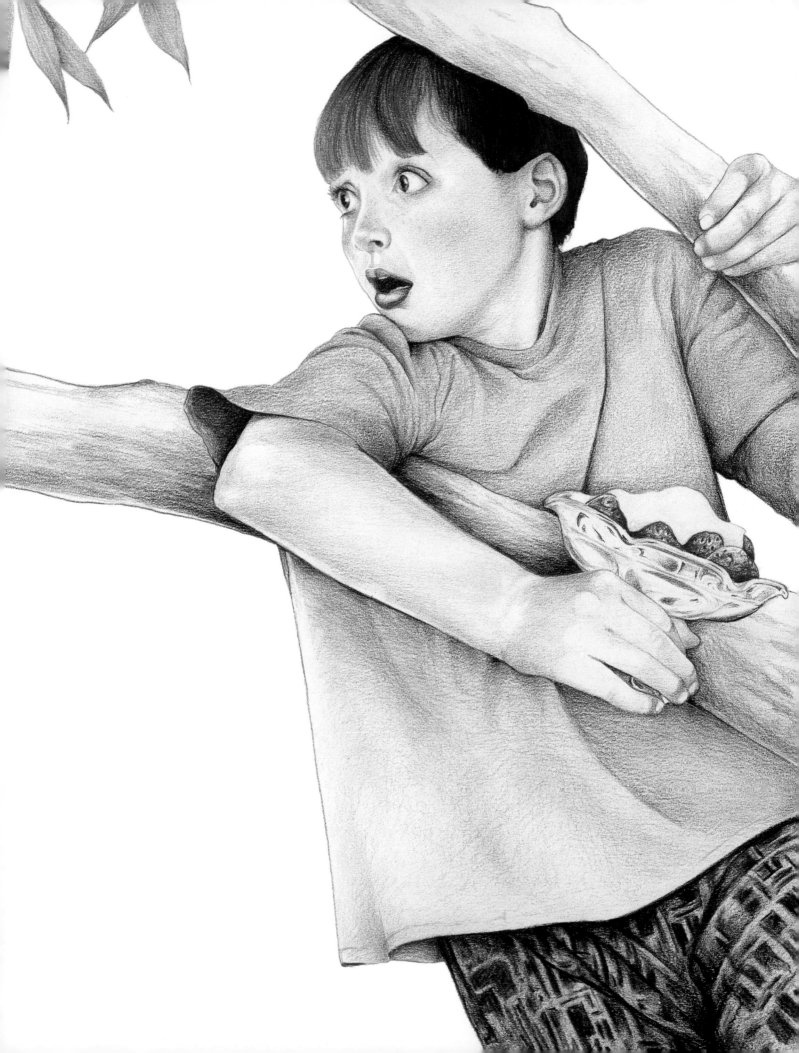

Skitty has magnetism all right.
It isn't only food she attracts,
she attracts people too.

There's no escaping
that magnetic look…

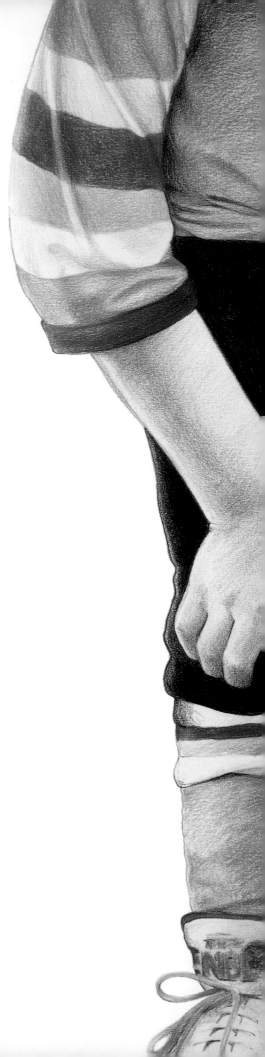

...that magnetic dog.